What Did We Do?

Before Cell Phones

by Samantha S. Bell

FOCUS READERS

BEACON

www.focusreaders.com

Focus Readers is distributed by North Star Editions:
sales@northstareditions.com | 888-417-0195

Produced for Focus Readers by Red Line Editorial.

Photographs ©: clearviewstock/Shutterstock Images, cover (left), 1 (left); sergey causelove/Shutterstock Images, cover (right), 1 (right); dvande/Shutterstock Images, 4; Savo Ilic/Shutterstock Images, 7; Everett Historical/Shutterstock Images, 8; whitemay/iStockphoto, 10; Paisit Teeraphatsakool/Shutterstock Images, 12; Jummie/iStockphoto, 15, 29; Ken Schulze/Shutterstock Images, 16–17; Africa Studio/Shutterstock Images, 18; Guy Shapira/Shutterstock Images, 21; Vasilyev Alexandr/Shutterstock Images, 23; thawornnurak/iStockphoto, 24; Anders/Wikimedia Commons, 27 (older phones); Vasin Lee/Shutterstock Images, 27 (iPhone)

Library of Congress Cataloging-in-Publication Data
Names: Bell, Samantha, author.
Title: Before cell phones / by Samantha S. Bell.
Description: Lake Elmo, MN : Focus Readers, 2020. | Series: What did we do? | Includes index. | Audience: Grades 4-6
Identifiers: LCCN 2019031729 (print) | LCCN 2019031730 (ebook) | ISBN 9781644930410 (hardcover) | ISBN 9781644931202 (paperback) | ISBN 9781644932780 (ebook pdf) | ISBN 9781644931998 (hosted ebook)
Subjects: LCSH: Telecommunication--History--Juvenile literature.
Classification: LCC TK5102.4 .B45 2020 (print) | LCC TK5102.4 (ebook) | DDC 384.09--dc23
LC record available at https://lccn.loc.gov/2019031729
LC ebook record available at https://lccn.loc.gov/2019031730

Printed in the United States of America
Mankato, MN
012020

About the Author

Samantha S. Bell is a children's writer and illustrator. She has written more than 100 nonfiction books for children. She enjoys using her cell phone, but she still needs to learn how to use some of the apps.

Table of Contents

Phone

Chapter 1

A Good Call

In 1976, Alfred spent a day at the pool. He was 12 years old. When Alfred was ready to go home, he called his mom to pick him up. Cell phones had not been invented yet. So, Alfred used a pay phone.

Before cell phones, people used pay phones when away from home.

Pay phones let people make calls from public places. People paid with coins. Then they could talk for a certain number of minutes.

Alfred put a dime into the pay phone's slot. He dialed his home's phone number. No one answered. So, Alfred hung up. He pushed a

Fun Fact

The first pay phone appeared in 1889. It stood on a street corner in Hartford, Connecticut.

In the United Kingdom, pay phones are often placed inside red booths.

lever to get his dime back. Then he tried calling again. Later, he returned home.

Chapter 2

Sending Messages

Cell phones let people call or send messages from almost anywhere. A response often comes back quickly. Before cell phones, getting in touch with people was not as easy. Many people sent letters.

Bags of mail traveled by ship or train to reach people's homes.

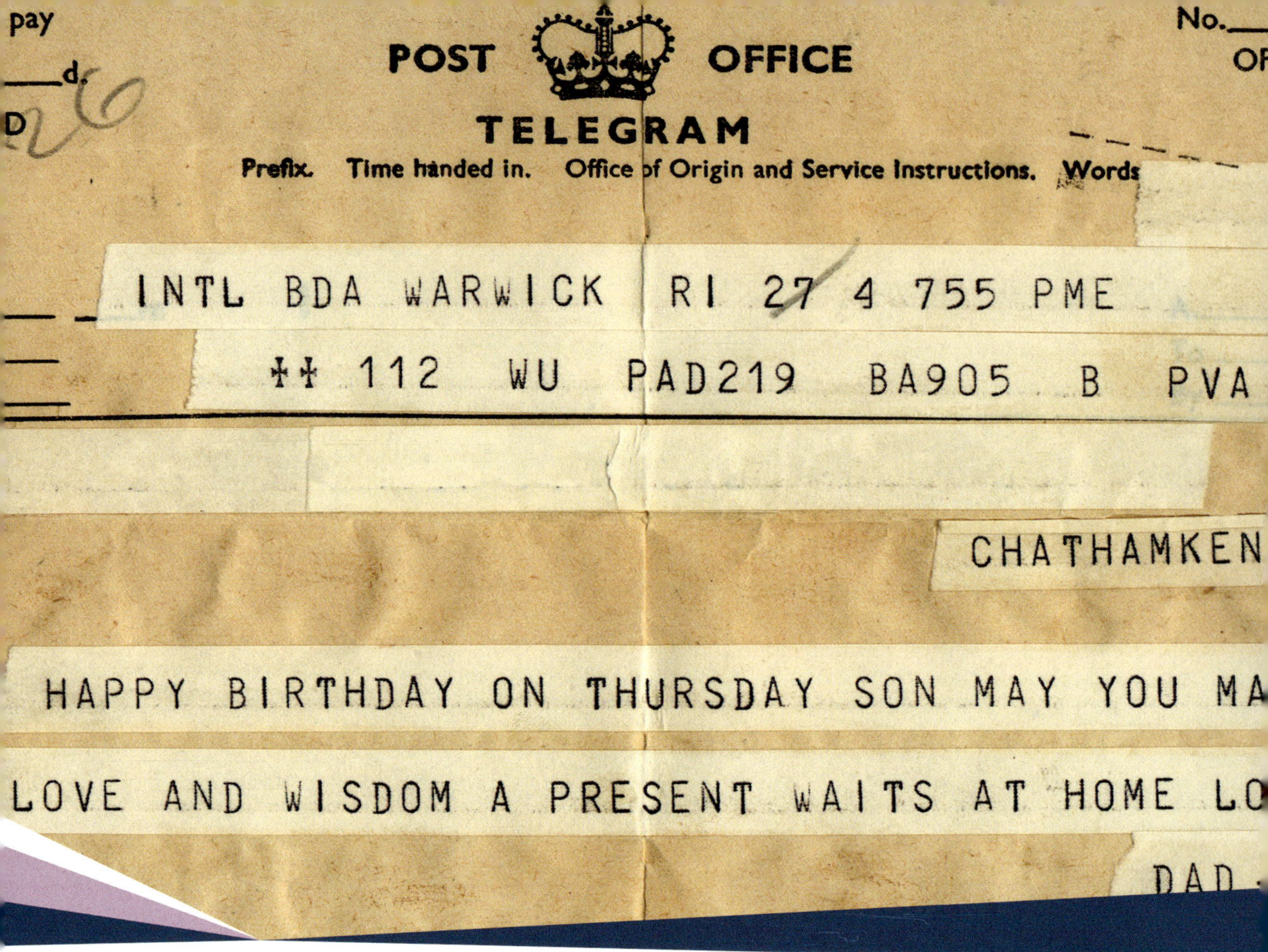
pay

____d.

D

POST OFFICE

TELEGRAM

Prefix. Time handed in. Office of Origin and Service Instructions. Words

No.____

OF

INTL BDA WARWICK RI 27 4 755 PME

++ 112 WU PAD219 BA905 B PVA

CHATHAMKEN

HAPPY BIRTHDAY ON THURSDAY SON MAY YOU MA

LOVE AND WISDOM A PRESENT WAITS AT HOME LO

DAD

Telegrams were a quick way to send short messages.

However, mail could take days or weeks to deliver.

In the mid-1800s, people began using **telegraphs**. First, the sender wrote a short message. An operator tapped out the message in code. The code was sent along wires or as radio signals. Another person listened to this code and wrote out the message. The message was called a telegram. Telegrams could reach people much faster than letters.

Fun Fact

Adding **punctuation** to a telegram cost extra. So, people used the word *stop* to mark the end of each sentence.

A rotary phone has a dial instead of buttons.

The telephone was invented in 1876. It let people talk directly to one another. To make a call, people picked up the **receiver**. They listened for a **dial tone**. Then they dialed the other person's number.

From the 1920s through the 1960s, people used rotary phones. These phones had a round dial. The dial had a hole for each number. Users put a finger in the hole for the number they wanted. Then they spun the dial. Later phones had buttons instead of dials.

Fun Fact

Very early phones didn't have numbers. Instead, callers talked to an operator. They told the operator where they wanted to call.

At first, all phones were landlines. Landlines are phones that use cables or wires to send signals. People plugged each phone in to a wall. A cable sent signals to wires outside. The wires carried signals to and from other phones.

The receiver connected to the rest of the phone with a cord. People could only go as far as the cord reached. Later, people began using cordless phones. But they still had to stay near the house.

Landlines use cables. They must plug in to a wall to make or receive calls.

When people were away from home, they used pay phones. Some pay phones hung on walls in stores or other buildings. Others were in booths on sidewalks.

BLAST FROM THE PAST

Party Lines

In the country, houses are more spread out. Giving each house a phone line could cost a lot. So, people often used party lines. A party line was one phone line that several customers shared. Each home had its own phone and a **distinct** ring. When someone called, people listened to the ring to see which home it was for.

A party line could only take one call at a time. While one person talked, the others had to wait. If they picked up their phones, they could hear what the other person was saying. Sometimes they listened in on purpose!

Telephone poles hold wires that connect to houses so people can use landlines.

Chapter 3

Different Devices

Today, people use cell phones for many tasks. They play music, take pictures, tell time, and much more. In the past, people had to use several different devices. They listened to music on radios.

Before cell phones, people often owned separate alarm clocks and radios.

Or they played **records**, **cassette tapes,** or CDs. People also used timers, watches, and alarm clocks.

When people needed directions, they used paper maps. They often kept maps in their cars. Sometimes people used a road atlas. It was a book of maps. Each map showed roads in a certain area. People turned the book's pages to see different areas. They could find where they were and where they wanted to go.

A GPS device displays directions on a screen.

To stay in touch when they traveled, people sent postcards. Postcards have pictures on one side. The other side has space for the address and a short note.

People often mailed the postcards to friends and family.

To take photos, people needed a camera. Before the 2000s, most cameras used film. Each roll of film could hold a certain number of photos. After taking pictures, people brought the film to a store.

Fun Fact

In the 1980s, pagers were popular. These devices used radio signals to send short messages.

Photo albums stored and protected printed pictures.

There, workers printed copies of the photos. People often kept the photos in albums. By the early 2000s, **digital** cameras became common. People began storing photos on their computers instead.

1
2 ABC
3 DEF
4 GHI
5 JKL
6 MNO
7 PRS
8 TUV
9 WXY
*
0 OPR
#
Rcl
Clr
Snd
Sto
Lock
End
Pwr
Vol

Chapter 4

Going Mobile

A few companies sold cell phones in the 1980s. But the phones were large and heavy. They also cost a lot. During the 1990s, cell phones became smaller and cheaper. More people began using them.

Early cell phones used antennas to send radio signals.

Early cell phones could only make calls. By the 1990s, people could send text messages. Soon, texting was more common than calling.

Smartphones were made in the early 2000s. These phones can access the internet. And they run **apps**. People can do many tasks right on their phones.

Fun Fact

The first cell phone weighed more than 2 pounds (0.9 kg).

PHONES THROUGH THE YEARS

Today, smartphones give people easy access to all kinds of information. People can share ideas with friends. Or they can play games. In fact, many people spend several hours each day on their phones.

Before Cell Phones

Write your answers on a separate piece of paper.

1. Write a sentence summarizing the main idea of Chapter 4.
2. Would you rather get a handwritten letter or a text message? Why?
3. Which invention did people use first?
   - **A.** telegraph
   - **B.** rotary phone
   - **C.** cell phone
4. What happened if someone talked for a long time on a party line?
   - **A.** The phone stopped working.
   - **B.** No one could hear what the person was saying.
   - **C.** No one else on the line could make a phone call.

5. What does **response** mean in this book?

*A **response** often comes back quickly. Before cell phones, getting in touch with people was not as easy.*

A. a question

B. a reply

C. an idea

6. What does **access** mean in this book?

*Smartphones were made in the early 2000s. These phones can **access** the internet.*

A. avoid

B. use

C. change

Answer key on page 32.

Glossary

apps
Computer programs that complete specific tasks.

cassette tapes
Small cases holding magnetic tape that can be used to record or play sounds.

dial tone
A sound that indicates a caller may start dialing a number.

digital
Having to do with information used on a computer.

distinct
Separate or different in obvious ways.

punctuation
Marks used in writing to separate parts of sentences or make the meaning clear.

receiver
The part of a telephone that the user holds and speaks into.

records
Flat disks that use tiny grooves to play sounds.

telegraphs
Machines that send messages over long distances using wires or radio signals.

To Learn More

BOOKS

Beevor, Lucy. *The Invention of the Telephone*. North Mankato, MN: Capstone Press, 2018.

Fraser, Mary Ann. *Alexander Graham Bell Answers the Call*. Watertown, MA: Charlesbridge, 2017.

Ward, Lesley. *Tech World: Cell Phone Pros and Cons*. Huntington Beach, CA: Teacher Created Materials, 2018.

NOTE TO EDUCATORS

Visit **www.focusreaders.com** to find lesson plans, activities, links, and other resources related to this title.

Index

Answer Key: 1. Answers will vary; **2.** Answers will vary; **3.** A; **4.** C; **5.** B; **6.** B